Mystery at MANZANAR

A WWII INTERNMENT CAMP STORY

by Eric Fein

illustrated by
Kurt Hartman

Librarian Reviewer
Laurie K. Holland
Media Specialist (National Board Certified), Edina, MN
MA in Elementary Education, Minnesota State University, Mankato

Reading Consultant
Elizabeth Stedem
Educator/Consultant, Colorado Springs, CO
MA in Elementary Education, University of Denver, CO

STONE ARCH BOOKS
www.stonearchbooks.com

Graphic Flash is published by Stone Arch Books
151 Good Counsel Drive, P.O. Box 669
Mankato, Minnesota 56002
www.stonearchbooks.com

Library of Congress Cataloging-in-Publication Data
Fein, Eric.
Mystery at Manzanar: A WWII Internment Camp Story / by Eric Fein; illustrated by Kurt Hartman.
p. cm. — (Graphic Flash)
ISBN 978-1-4342-0751-7 (library binding : alk. paper)
ISBN 978-1-4342-0847-7 (pbk. : alk. paper)
1. Graphic novels. [1. Graphic novels. 2. Japanese Americans—Evacuation and relocation, 1942–1945—Fiction. 3. Manzanar War Relocation Center—Fiction. 4. Mystery and detective stories.] I. Hartman, Kurt, ill. II. Title.
PZ7.7.F45My 2009
[Fic]—dc22 2008006669

Summary: During World War II, 15-year-old Tommy Yamamoto and his family are forced into the Manzanar interment camp for Japanese Americans. While there, an elderly internee is attacked, and one of the camp's guards is charged with the crime. Tommy sets out to solve the crime and discovers some unlikely suspects.

Art Director: Heather Kindseth
Graphic Designer: Brann Garvey

1 2 3 4 5 6 13 12 11 10 09 08

Printed in the United States of America

Table of Contents

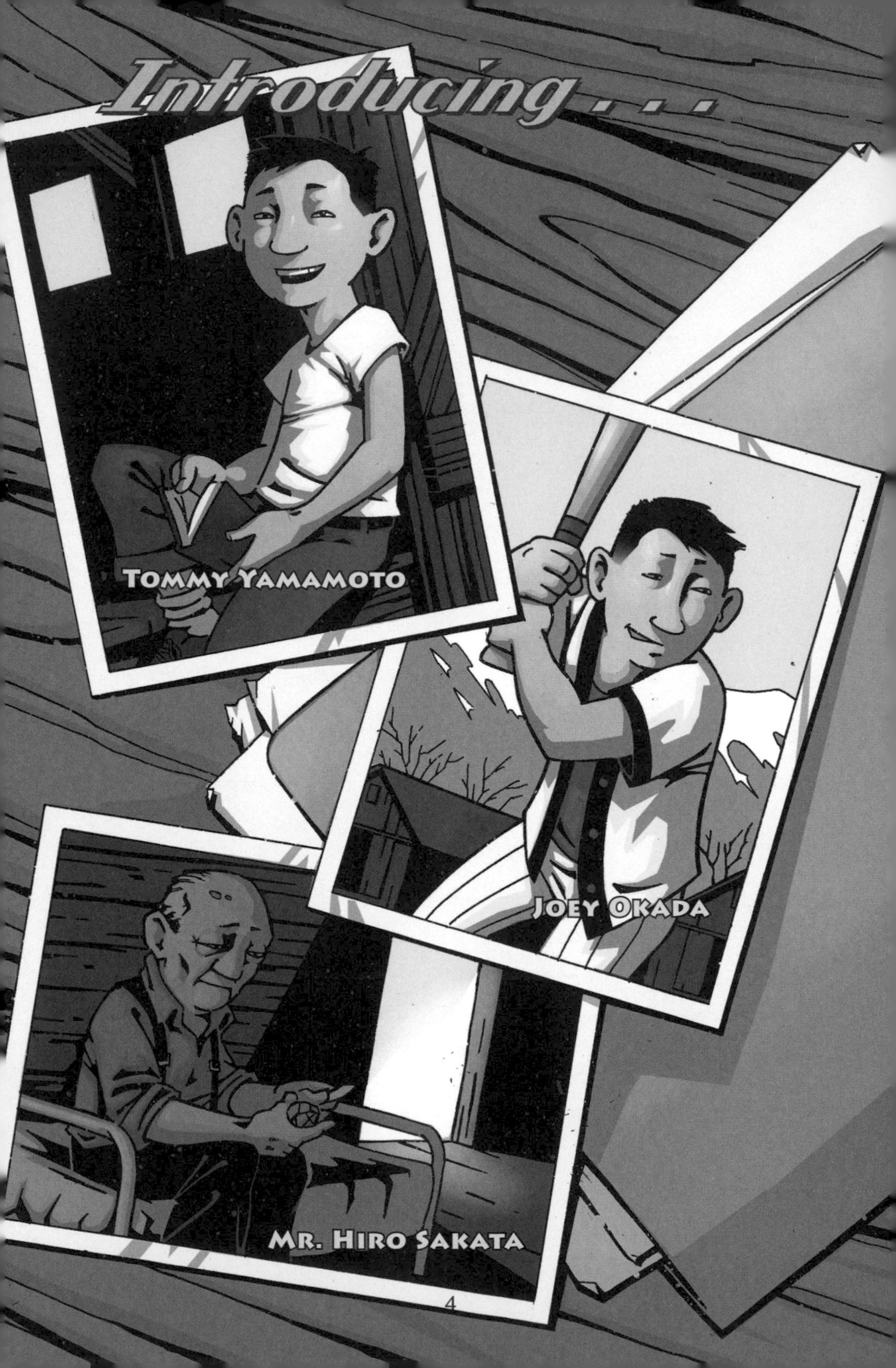

Introducing . . .
Tommy Yamamoto
Joey Okada
Mr. Hiro Sakata

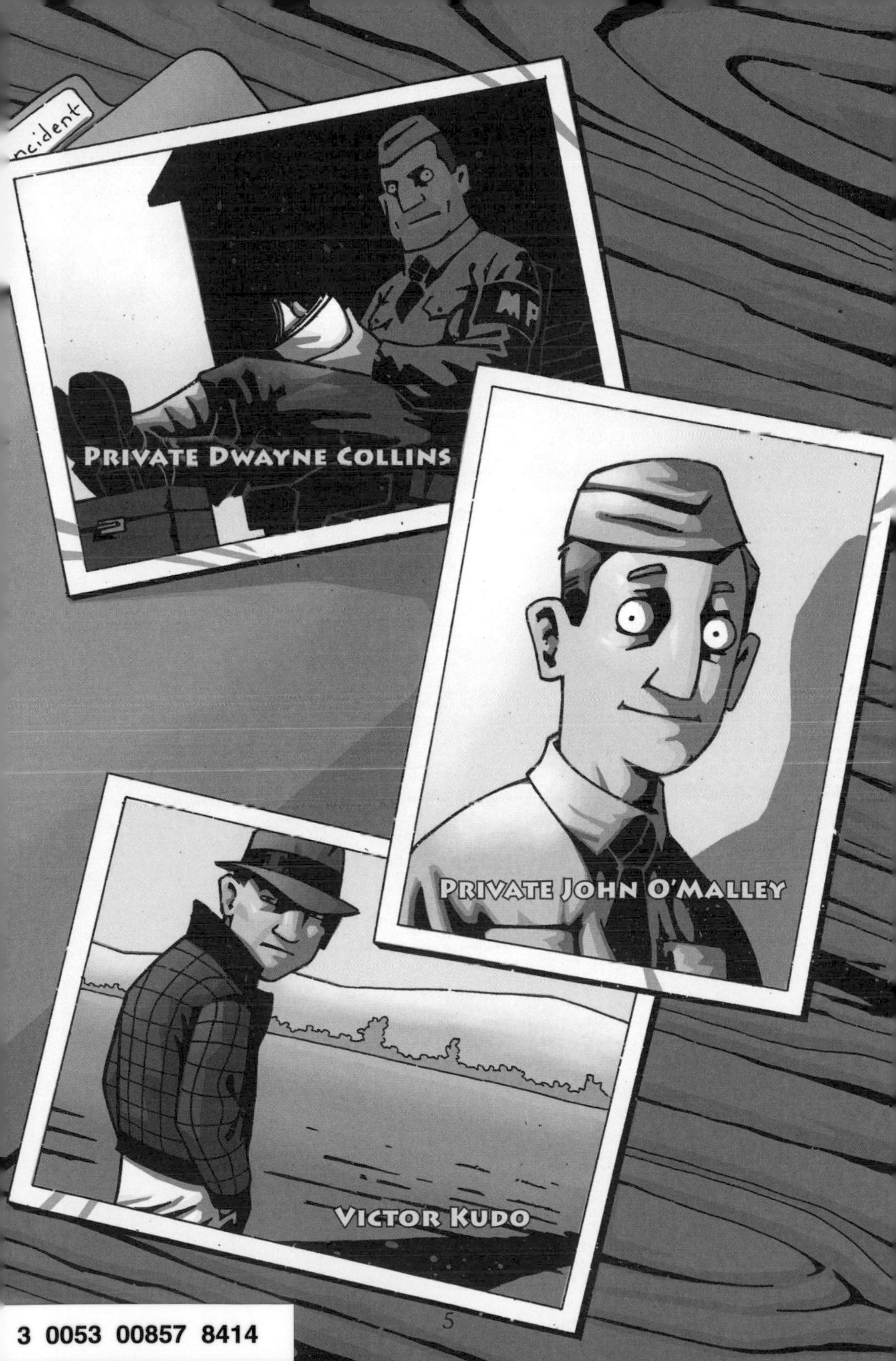
ncident
MP
PRIVATE DWAYNE COLLINS
PRIVATE JOHN O'MALLEY
VICTOR KUDO

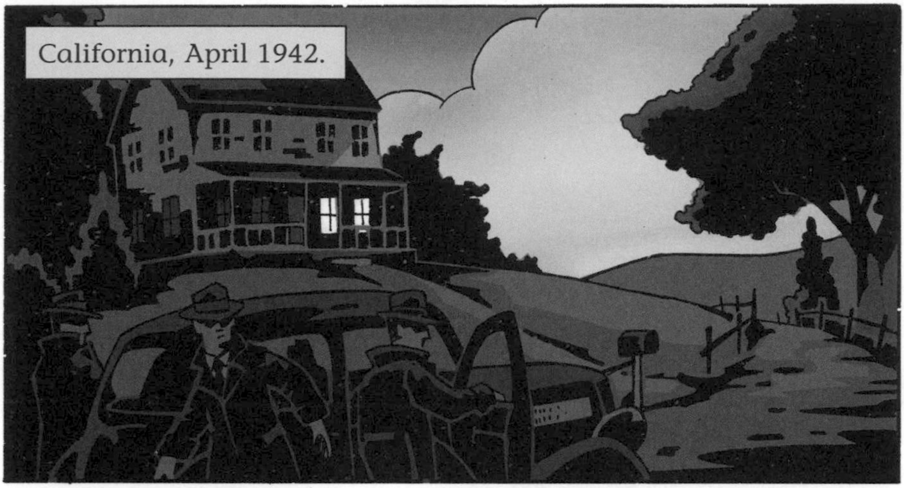
California, April 1942.

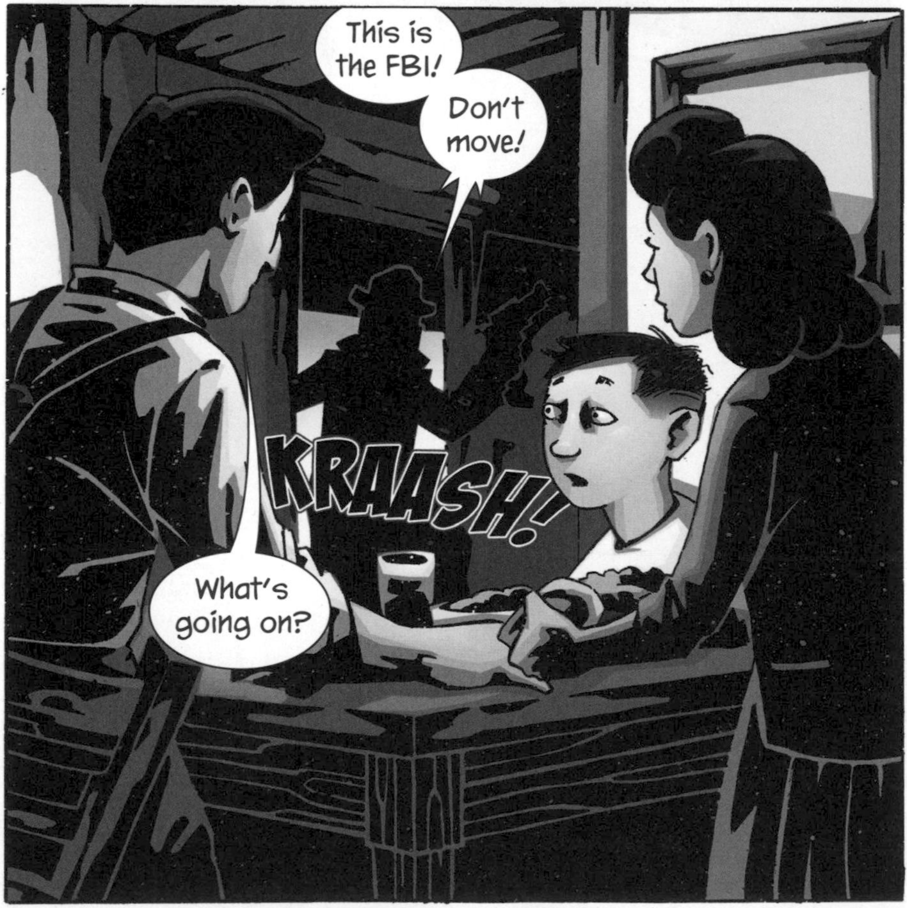
This is the FBI!
Don't move!
KRAAASH!
What's going on?

CHAPTER 1

Taken Captive

They came as we were having dinner. They didn't bother to knock. Ever since the attack on Pearl Harbor, the United States government didn't trust Japanese Americans. Now, they were going to take us away.

My parents came to America in 1915. They had little money but managed to buy a small farm. They wanted to raise a family and live as Americans. However, because my parents are *Issei*, meaning they were born in Japan, they are not allowed to become American citizens. My sister, Mary, and I are *Nisei*. We were born here in California. We are legal citizens of the United States. Sadly, most Americans view us as outsiders. They see danger in our faces.

"What right do you have to break into my home?" my father yelled.

"I'm Agent Fisk. The War Department ordered us to search this house," the man replied.

For the next three hours, the agents tore apart our home. A couple of them seemed to enjoy making a mess of our things. In the end, they found nothing. I don't know what they expected to find. My parents were farmers, not spies.

"Good work, men," Agent Fisk said. "Take Mr. Yamamoto to the office so we can question him some more."

"No! My husband has done nothing wrong," Mother shouted.

"I have my orders," said Agent Fisk. "All Japanese on the West Coast of the United States are being moved inland for national security."

As the agents grabbed my father's arm, my mother started to cry. My father looked at her with a sad smile. "Easy, Tamiko," he said. "I'll be fine."

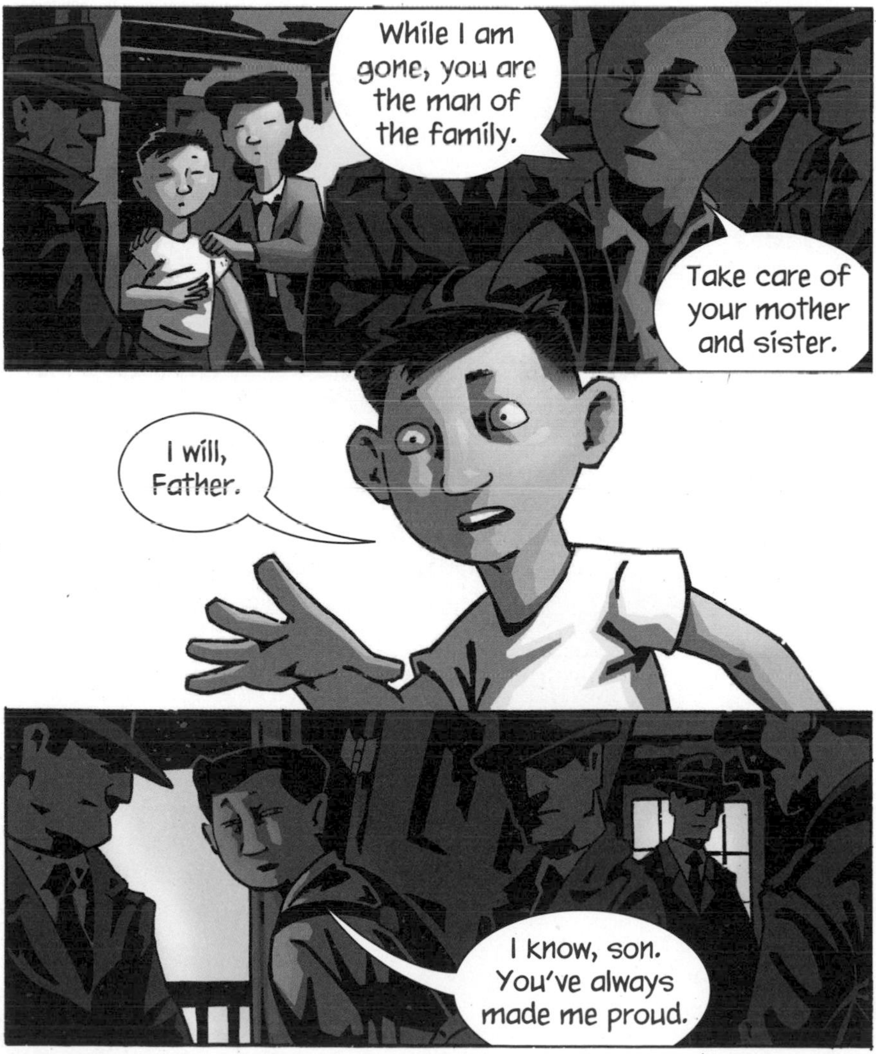
While I am gone, you are the man of the family.
Take care of your mother and sister.
I will, Father.
I know, son. You've always made me proud.

The next two weeks were a blur. We were told that we were being moved for our own good. We weren't told where we were going. We could only take what we could carry. Everything else was sold or put in storage with neighbors.

Besides my clothes, the only thing I packed was a book. It was a collection of Sherlock Holmes mystery stories. I loved reading them. Sherlock Holmes always based his conclusions on cold hard facts. That was something the rest of the world seemed unable to do at the moment.

Our family first went to an assembly center. This was a place used to house thousands of Japanese Americans being removed from their homes. Our assembly center was a racetrack. We had to live in a stall where horses had been kept. It was cramped and smelly. After a month, we were sent to a camp that would be our new home.

It was a long, hot train ride to the camp. Each time the train went through a town, the people there yelled hateful things at us.

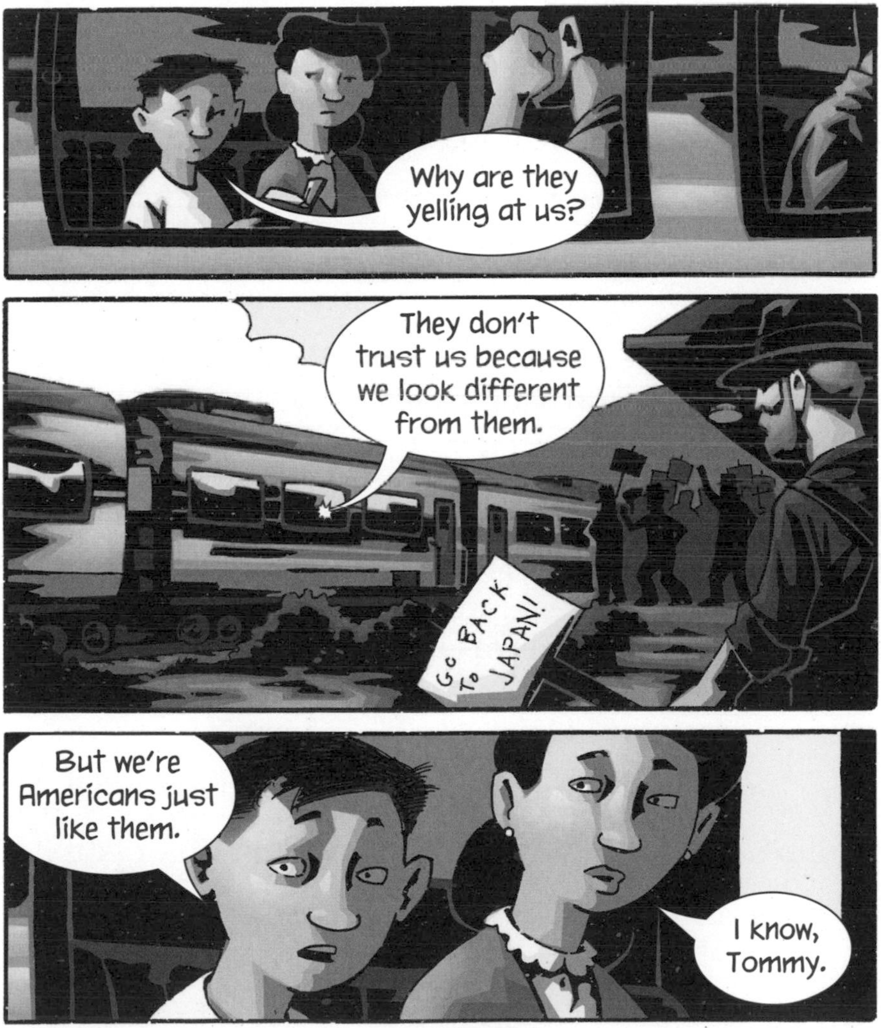
Why are they yelling at us?
They don't trust us because we look different from them.
GO BACK TO JAPAN!
But we're Americans just like them.
I know, Tommy.

CHAPTER 2

Manzanar

Days later, we arrived at the camp, the Manzanar Relocation Center. It was in the California desert, miles from any town. A fence topped with barbed wire surrounded the area.

There were two guard towers at the front and back of the camp. Guards with machine guns stood in the towers watching over us. The first time I saw them, it gave me an ice-cold knot in the pit of my stomach. It wasn't just the guns that made them scary. It was the angry look on their faces.

Despite the armed guards, our families settled into a daily routine at Manzanar. Adults got jobs in the camp. Children went to school.

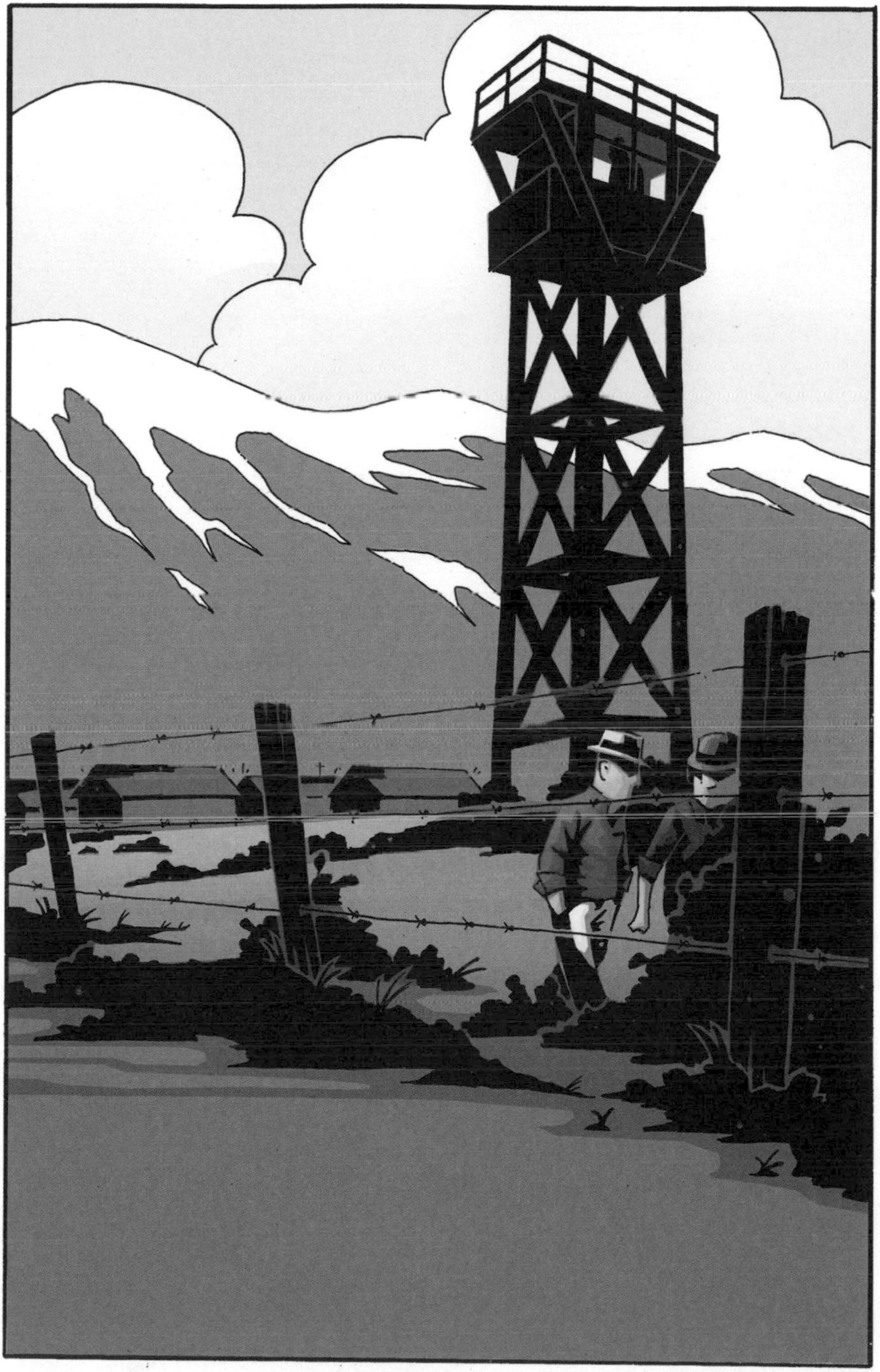

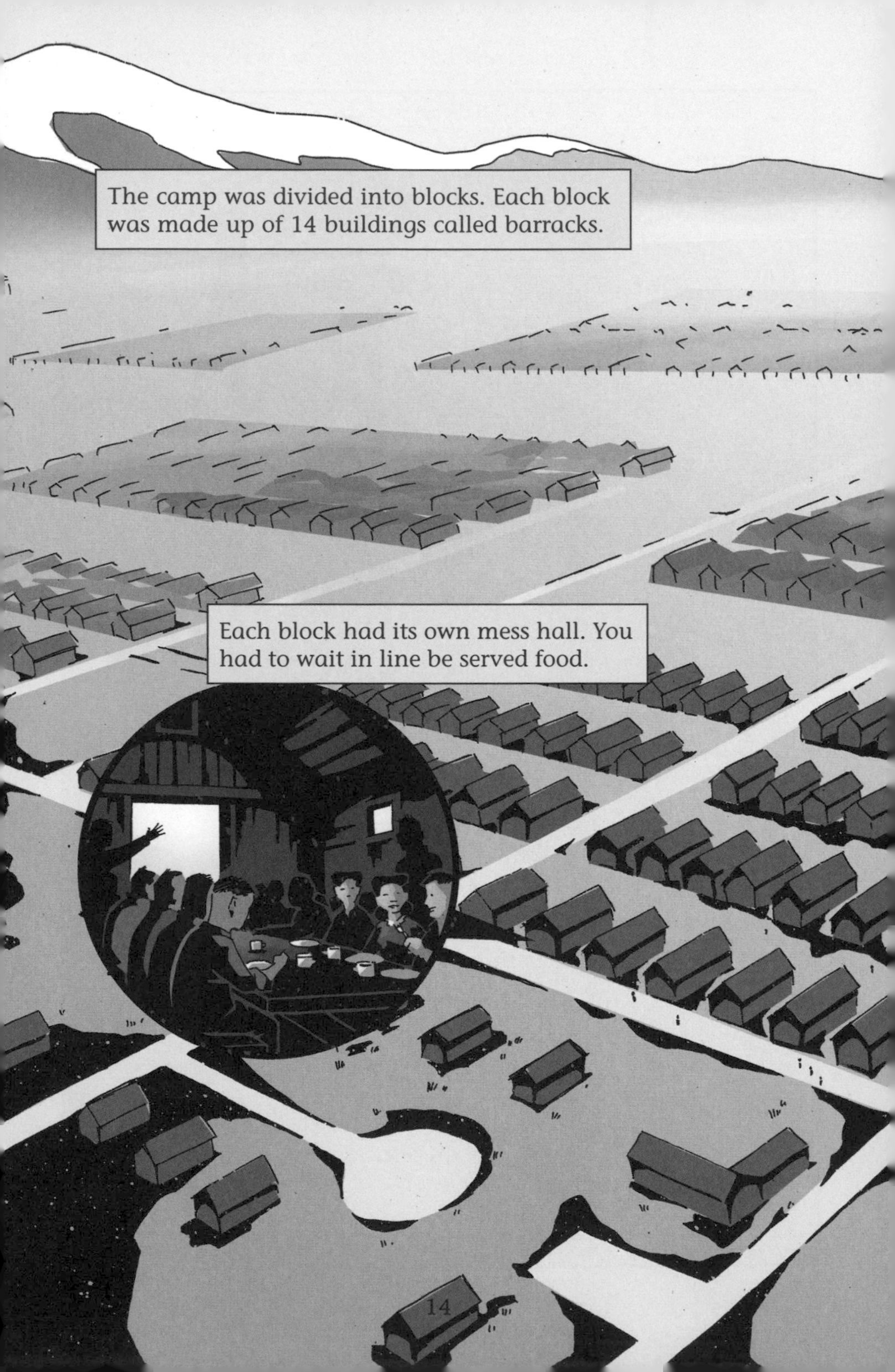
The camp was divided into blocks. Each block was made up of 14 buildings called barracks.
Each block had its own mess hall. You had to wait in line be served food.

Some people worked together to grow fresh fruit and vegetables for the camp.

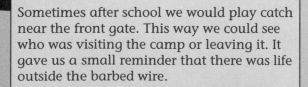

Sometimes after school we would play catch near the front gate. This way we could see who was visiting the camp or leaving it. It gave us a small reminder that there was life outside the barbed wire.

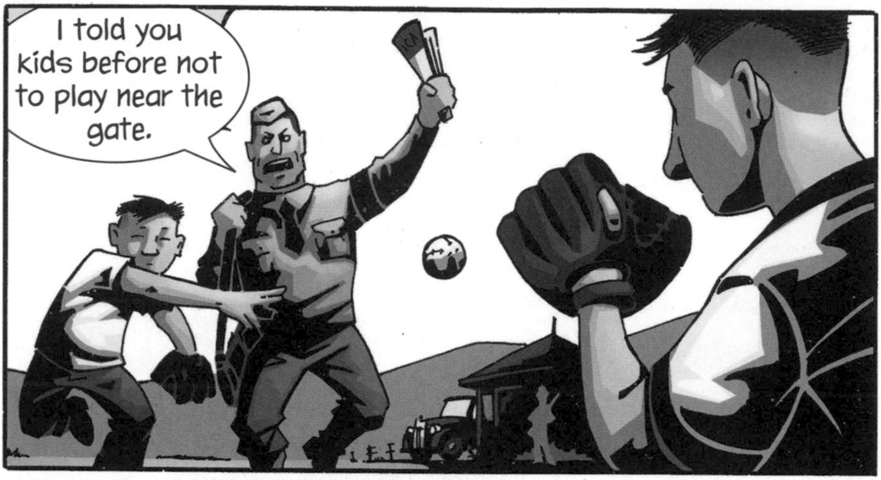
I told you kids before not to play near the gate.

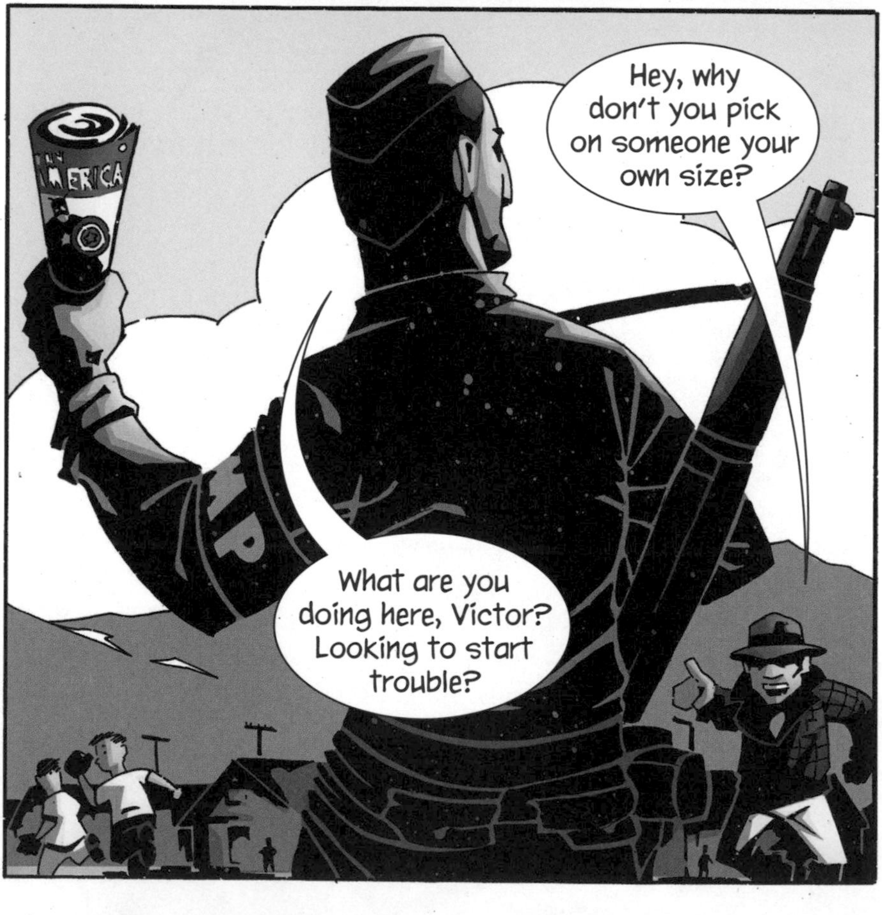
Hey, why don't you pick on someone your own size?
What are you doing here, Victor? Looking to start trouble?
AMERICA
MP

Some of the guards were nice. Others were nasty. Dwayne Collins was one of the nasty ones. Victor Kudo, one of the older boys at school, hated them all. He was always looking for a fight. When that happened, my friend Joey and I didn't stick around.

Sometimes, Victor got in fights at school when he called another boy an *inu*. I knew that *inu* was the Japanese word for dog. I didn't understand why that made people so angry.

"An *inu* is an informer," Joey explained to me one day. "It's someone who works on the side of the guards. Not on our side."

"I thought we were all on the same side," I said. "Aren't we all Americans?"

CHAPTER 3

The Crime

One morning, Joey and I stopped to chat with our neighbor, Mr. Sakata. Mr. Sakata was sitting in front of his barracks carving something out of a piece of wood. Since coming to the camp, he had carved about fifteen figurines. He kept them proudly displayed on a tiny shelf above his bed.

"What are you carving today?" Joey asked.

"A bald eagle," Mr. Sakata said. "It's the symbol of our country." Even though the government had sent him here to Manzanar, he could not find it in his heart to hate America.

"Wow, that's swell," Joey said. "Can I hold it?"

Mr. Sakata smiled. "Maybe when it's finished."

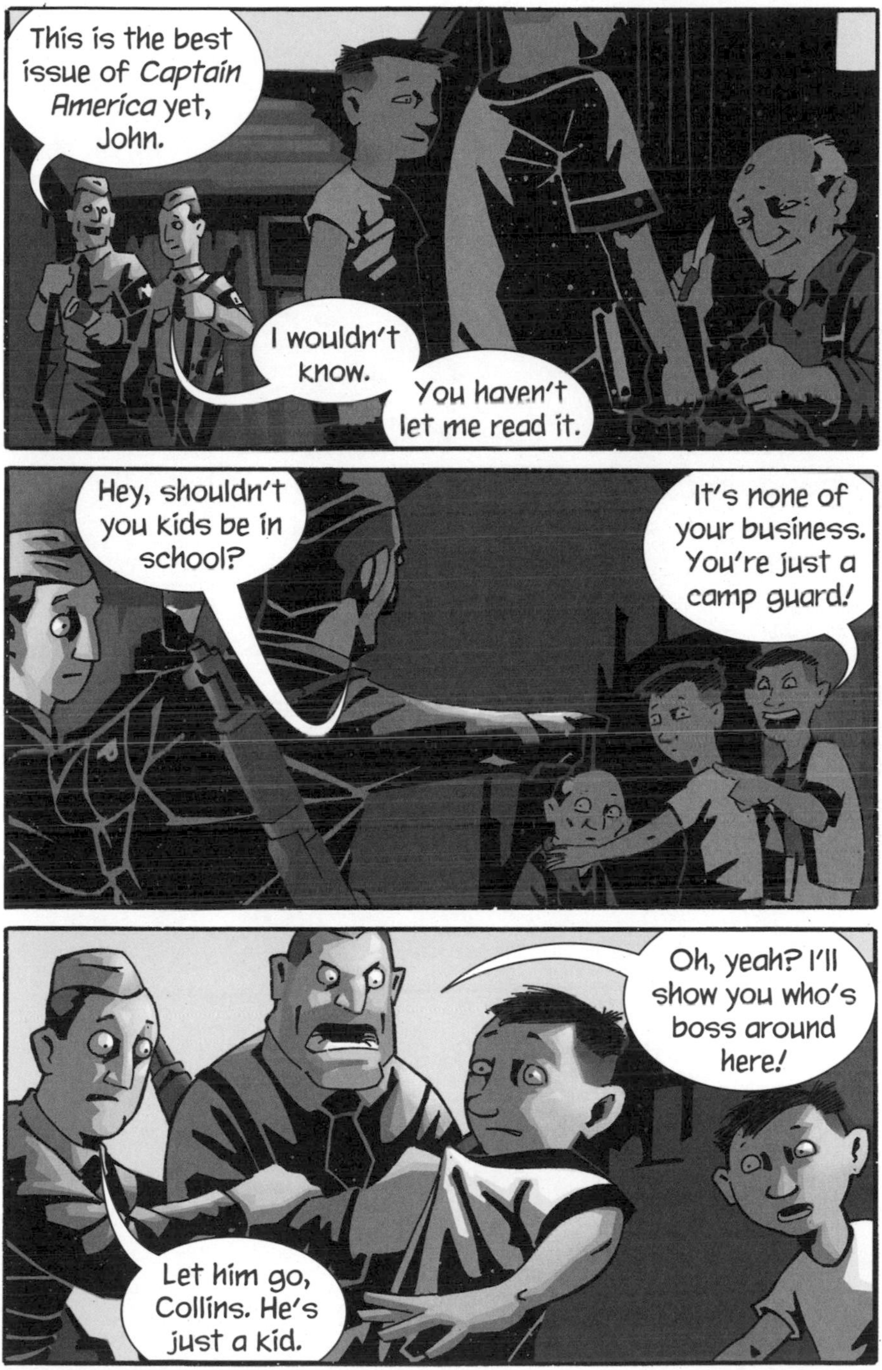
This is the best issue of *Captain America* yet, John.
I wouldn't know.
You haven't let me read it.
Hey, shouldn't you kids be in school?
It's none of your business. You're just a camp guard!
Oh, yeah? I'll show you who's boss around here!
Let him go, Collins. He's just a kid.

After school, I went right back to my family's quarters and stayed in my bed, reading.

"Tommy, it is time for dinner," Mother said.

"I'm not hungry," I said.

She sat on the edge of my bed and placed her hand on my forehead. "Do you have a fever?"

"No," I said.

She saw I was reading my Sherlock Holmes book again. "You read too many mysteries," she said. "They have too much violence. They make you upset. That's why you have no appetite."

"No, mom," I said. "I'm just not hungry."

"After dinner, do you want to go to a movie at the mess hall?" she asked.

"Nah. I just don't feel like it today," I said.

"Okay," she said. "I'll let you have your way this time."

I had seen the notice earlier in the day saying that a Roy Rogers western was going to be shown. Usually, I liked cowboy movies. But after running into Collins twice, I didn't want to risk a third.

Through the open window, I could hear Mr. Sakata hum as he put the finishing touches on his carving. I kept reading my Sherlock Holmes book.

Reading let me forget my troubles. After a few pages, I wasn't in an internment camp. Instead, I was with Sherlock Holmes chasing criminals through the foggy streets of London.

But then . . .

What was that?

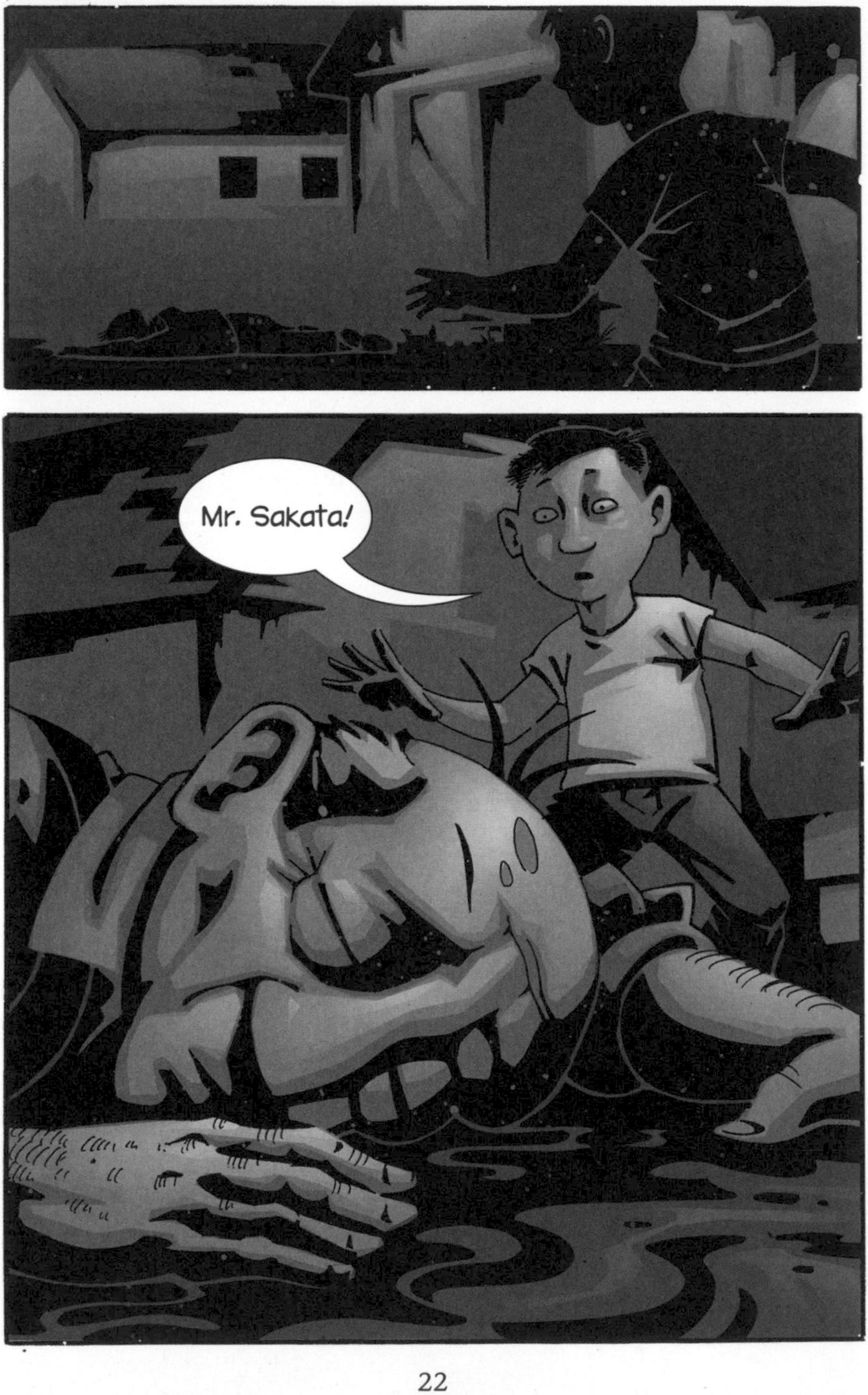
Mr. Sakata!

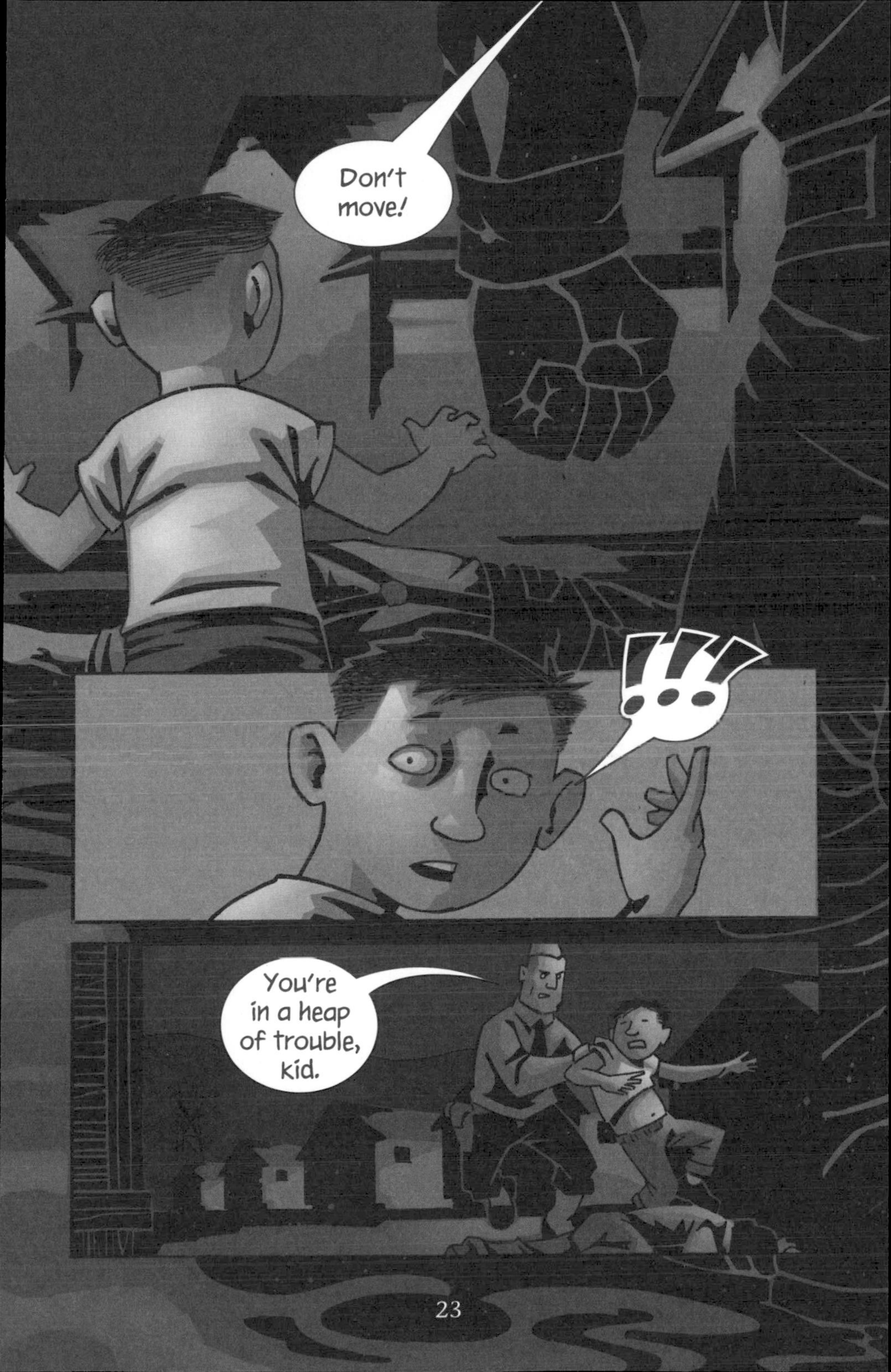
Don't move!
You're in a heap of trouble, kid.

CHAPTER 4

Under Suspicion

I was taken before the camp's head security officer. Representatives from my barracks' block joined him. I was scared. I really wished my father could be here with me. But we still didn't know where he was or if we would ever hear from him again. I reminded myself that I was the man of the family, and I would have to fix this situation myself.

Collins and John were standing on either side of me. Collins had just finished telling his version of events. Of course, he eagerly painted me as the attacker.

"How is Mr. Sakata doing?" asked the security officer.

"We took him over to the infirmary," John said. "Doc says he got a few bruises. He's going to keep him overnight for observation. Sakata should be okay in a day or two."

The security officer nodded, then looked at me.

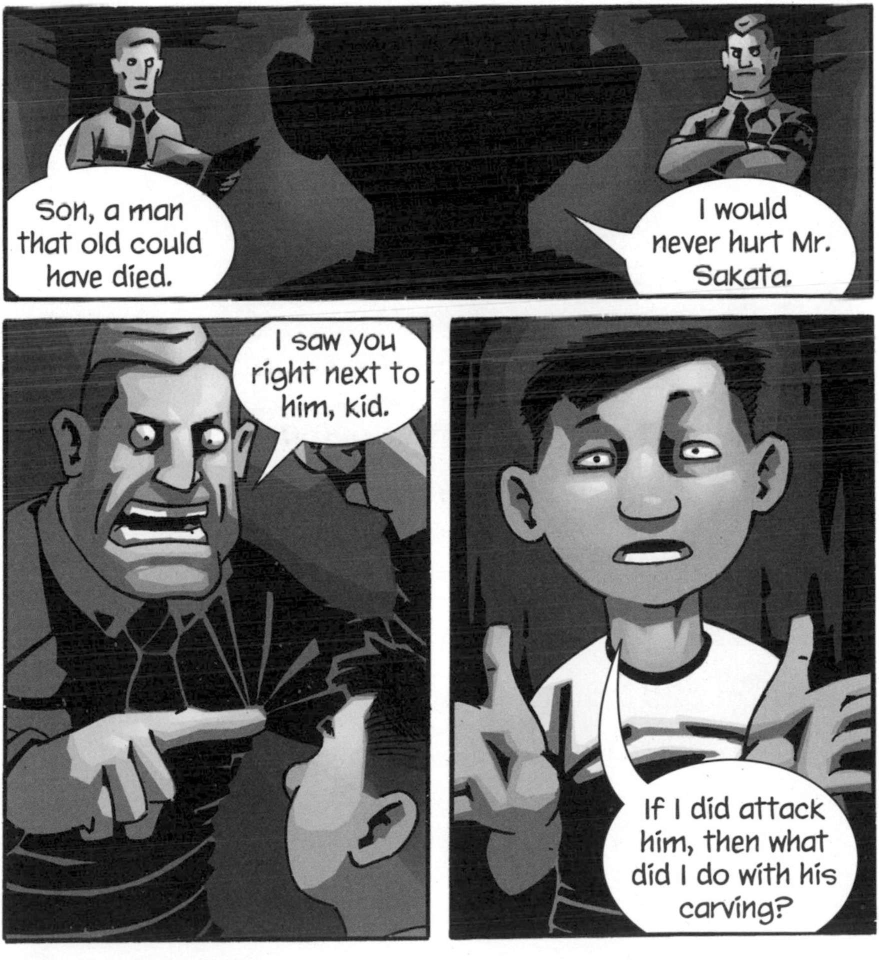
Son, a man that old could have died.
I would never hurt Mr. Sakata.
I saw you right next to him, kid.
If I did attack him, then what did I do with his carving?

"You could have thrown it into the bushes or hidden it somewhere nearby," Collins said.

"Sir, I really don't think Tommy did this," said John. "I've seen him with Mr. Sakata several times, and they get along pretty well."

"I want a search team set up to see if this carving can be found," the security officer said. "In the meantime, Private O'Malley, I want you to take this young man back to his barracks. He will stay there until we can figure this out."

The security officer looked me straight in the eye and said, "If you cause any more trouble, son, you'll leave me no choice but to have you locked up. Understand?"

"Yes, sir," I said quietly. John took me by the arm and led me outside. As the door closed behind us, he let go.

"Thanks for standing up for me," I said.

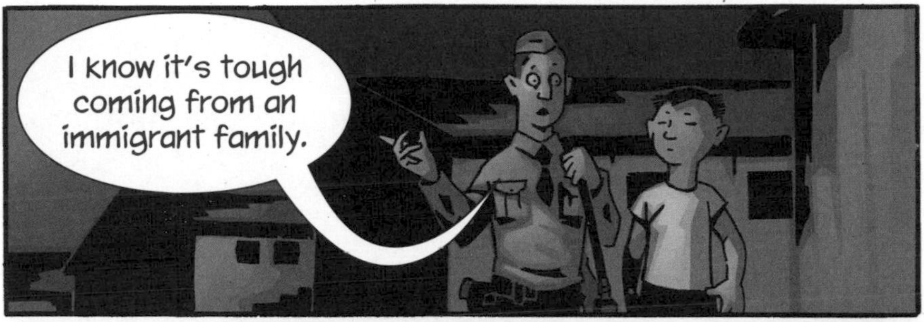
I know it's tough coming from an immigrant family.

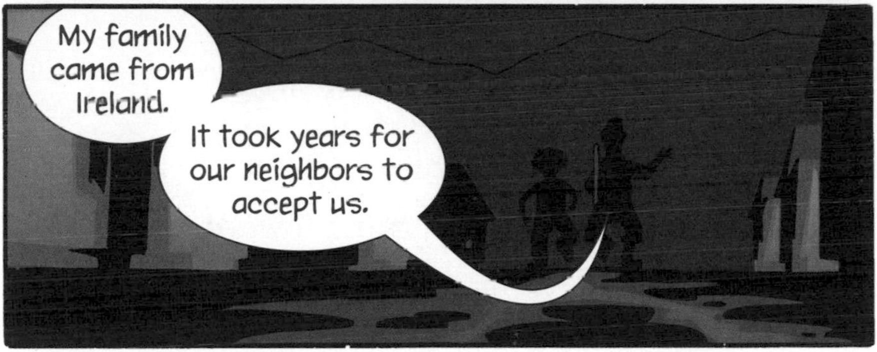
My family came from Ireland.
It took years for our neighbors to accept us.

When I got home, my mother was waiting. She was very upset. News of what happened to Mr. Sakata had spread like wildfire throughout the camp. She was afraid that I would be sent away.

Later that night, we were woken up by a loud knock at the door. *Were the guards coming back for me?* I wondered.

"Victor! What are you doing here?" my mother exclaimed as she opened the door.

"I have to talk to Tommy about what happened last night," he said.

"My son is innocent!" Mother shouted. "He would never hurt another person!"

"I know," Victor said, turning toward me. "It was John O'Malley, the camp guard."

"Huh?" I couldn't believe my ears. "It couldn't have been John. He treats us better than any of the guards."

"They found Mr. Sakata's carving in his locker," Victor said. "It was just another trick to keep us in line."

"What will happen to John?" I asked.

"He'll probably be sent to jail," he replied. "For now, he's been confined to his quarters."

"I have to speak to the security officer," I said.

"Why?" Victor asked, puzzled.

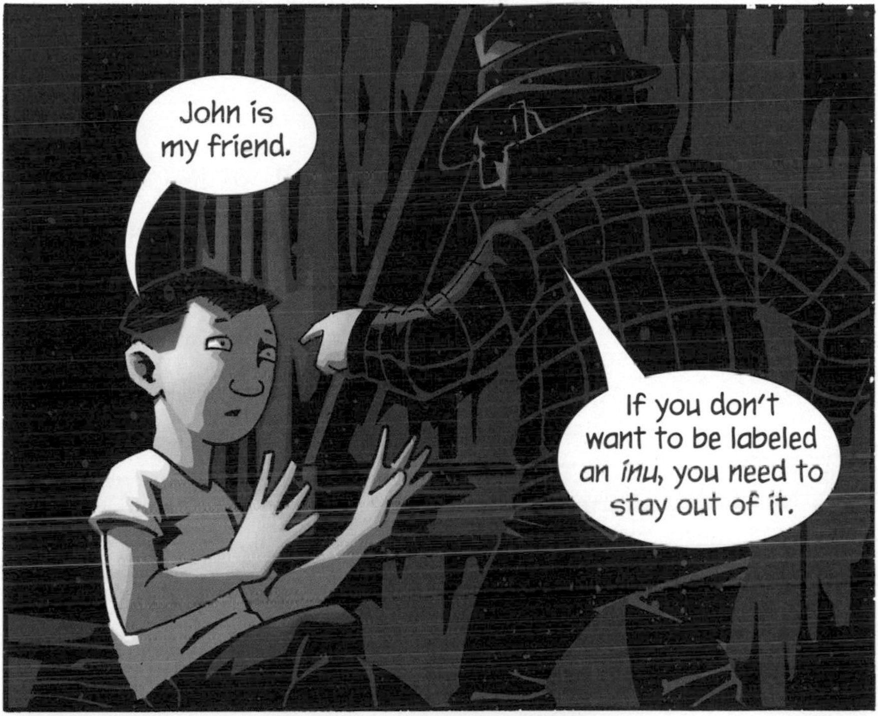

John is my friend.
If you don't want to be labeled an *inu*, you need to stay out of it.

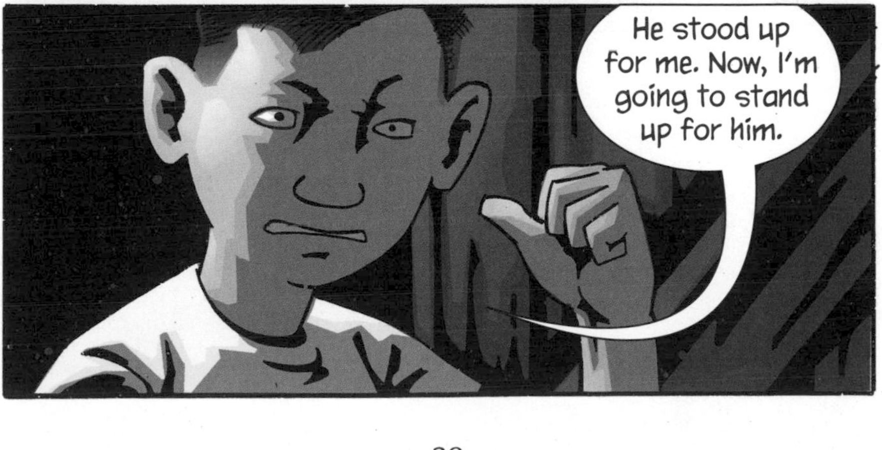

He stood up for me. Now, I'm going to stand up for him.

CHAPTER 5

Tommy Investigates

Early the next morning, I caught up with the head security officer as he was walking toward his office. "Son, you are giving me a headache," he said. "This case is closed."

"I'm sorry, sir," I said. "But I know that John O'Malley couldn't have attacked Mr. Sakata."

"You have any proof?" he asked.

"No, sir," I replied. "I just know that he didn't do it. What reason would he have to hurt Mr. Sakata?"

"I don't know," the officer said, turning to walk away. "But I can't have a guard in this camp that everyone thinks is dangerous. We've already had one riot here. I don't want another."

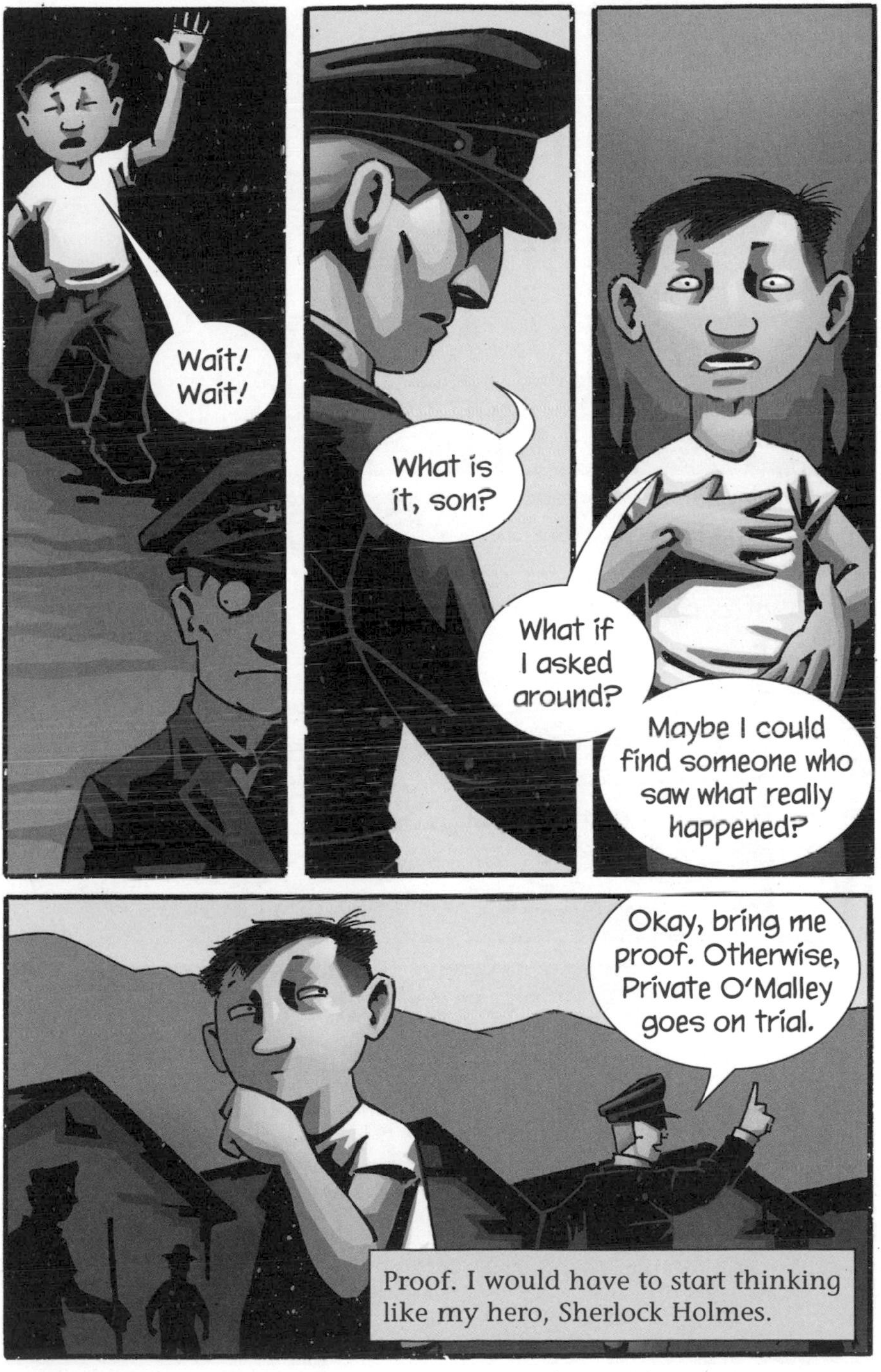
Wait!
Wait!
What is it, son?
What if I asked around?
Maybe I could find someone who saw what really happened?
Okay, bring me proof. Otherwise, Private O'Malley goes on trial.
Proof. I would have to start thinking like my hero, Sherlock Holmes.

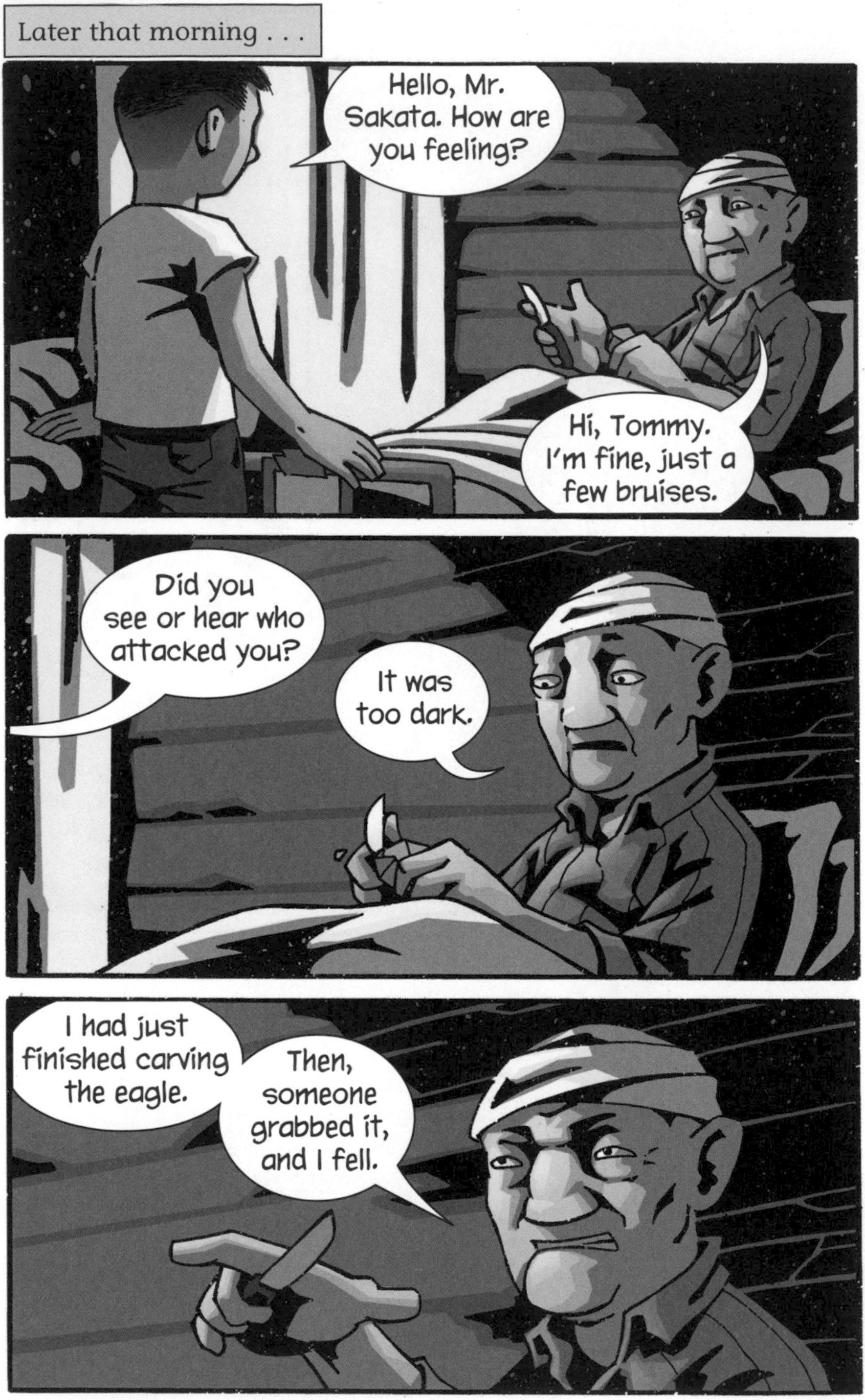
Later that morning . . .
Hello, Mr. Sakata. How are you feeling?
Hi, Tommy. I'm fine, just a few bruises.
Did you see or hear who attacked you?
It was too dark.
I had just finished carving the eagle.
Then, someone grabbed it, and I fell.

"It happened so quickly. I never saw who it was," Mr. Sakata continued. "My wife told me that one of the guards did it."

"Yes, John O'Malley," I said. "But I think that they got the wrong person."

"What are you saying?" Mr. Sakata asked.

"I know that John would never do something so terrible," I replied. "He is a good man."

"A good man does not attack people and take their belongings," he said.

"But there's no proof. And it just doesn't make any sense," I said. "Besides, it's only a rumor."

"I will not speak about this anymore," he said, pointing toward the door.

"I'm sorry, Mr. Sakata," I said.

Next, I went to find Collins. He was on duty at the front gate.

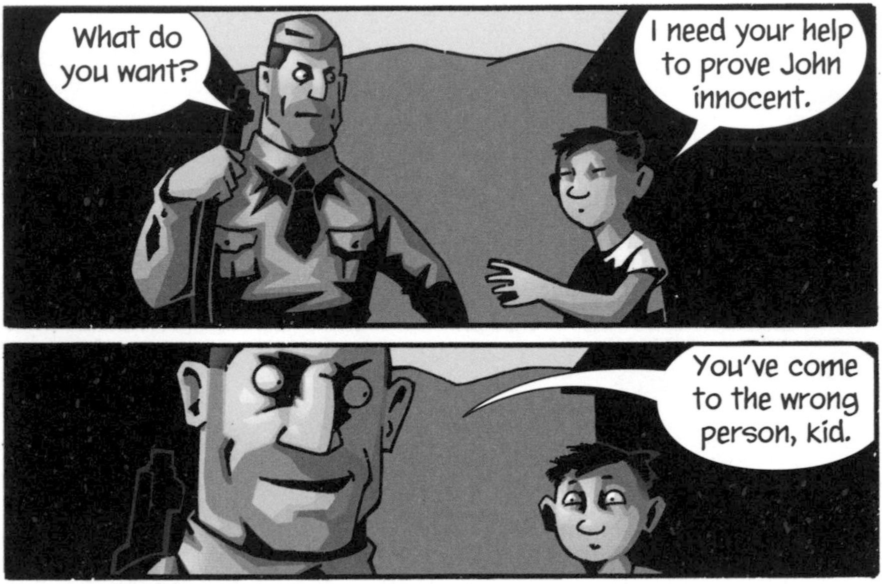
What do you want?
I need your help to prove John innocent.
You've come to the wrong person, kid.

"I thought John was your friend," I asked.

"Nah, he's just someone to talk to," Collins replied. "Who else am I going to talk to in this dustbowl? You?

"Last time I saw John, he was in the mess hall having dinner. I left him there to go on duty. That was a good hour before the attack."

I left feeling totally discouraged. Then, as I headed for dinner, Victor and his two friends spotted me. "Hey!" Victor yelled. "Are you trying to help clear the guard?"

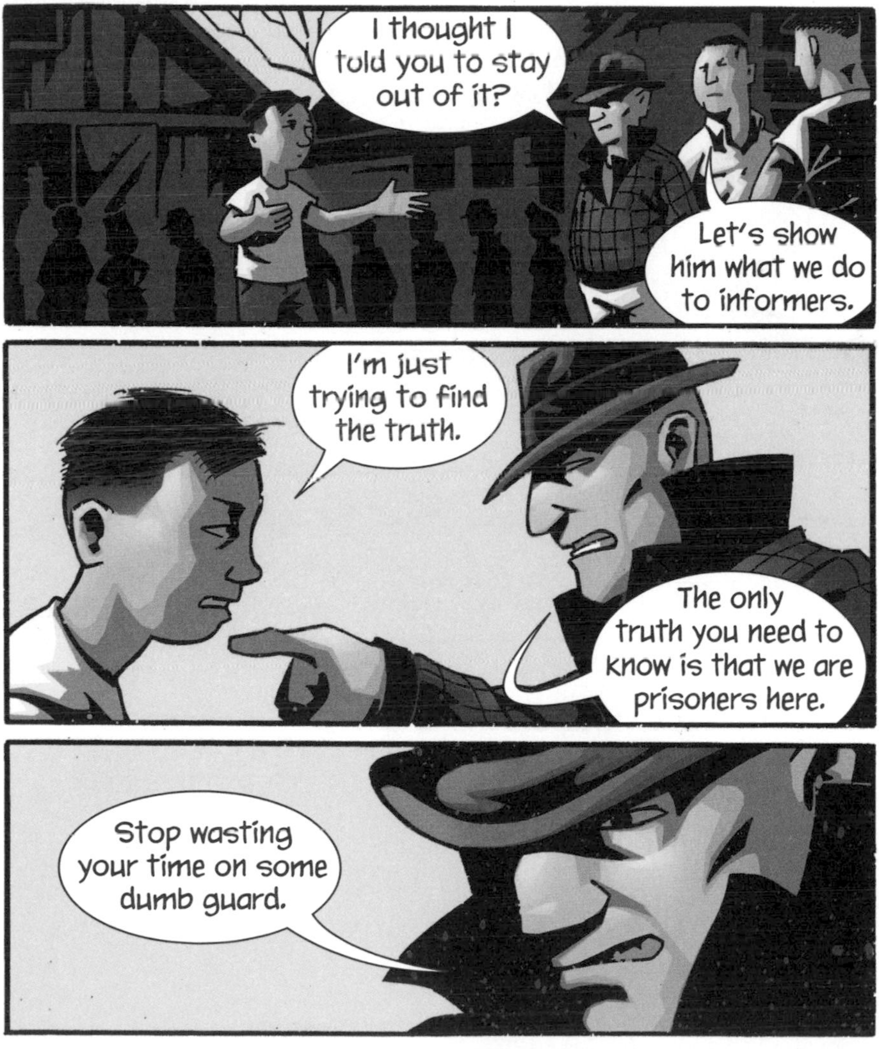
I thought I told you to stay out of it?
Let's show him what we do to informers.
I'm just trying to find the truth.
The only truth you need to know is that we are prisoners here.
Stop wasting your time on some dumb guard.

Dusting myself off, I realized that I hadn't gotten any closer to solving the case. No one seemed to have any answers. Now Victor and his friends weren't going to make this case any easier. I needed to hear John's side of the story. Maybe he could help rule out some of the suspects.

On the way to the officers' barracks, I ran into Joey. He was wearing his mitt and his baseball cleats. I had been so busy, I completely forgot about the baseball game.

"How'd the game go?" I asked.

"We could have used you," he replied. "You're the best shortstop in our block. What are you up to anyway?"

"Trying to find out what really happened to Mr. Sakata," I said. "You were at the movies last night. Did you see anything?"

Joey stared at his glove. After a moment, he looked up and answered.

"Nope," he said. "I was just watching the movie. Roy Rogers westerns are my favorite."

"I see," I said.

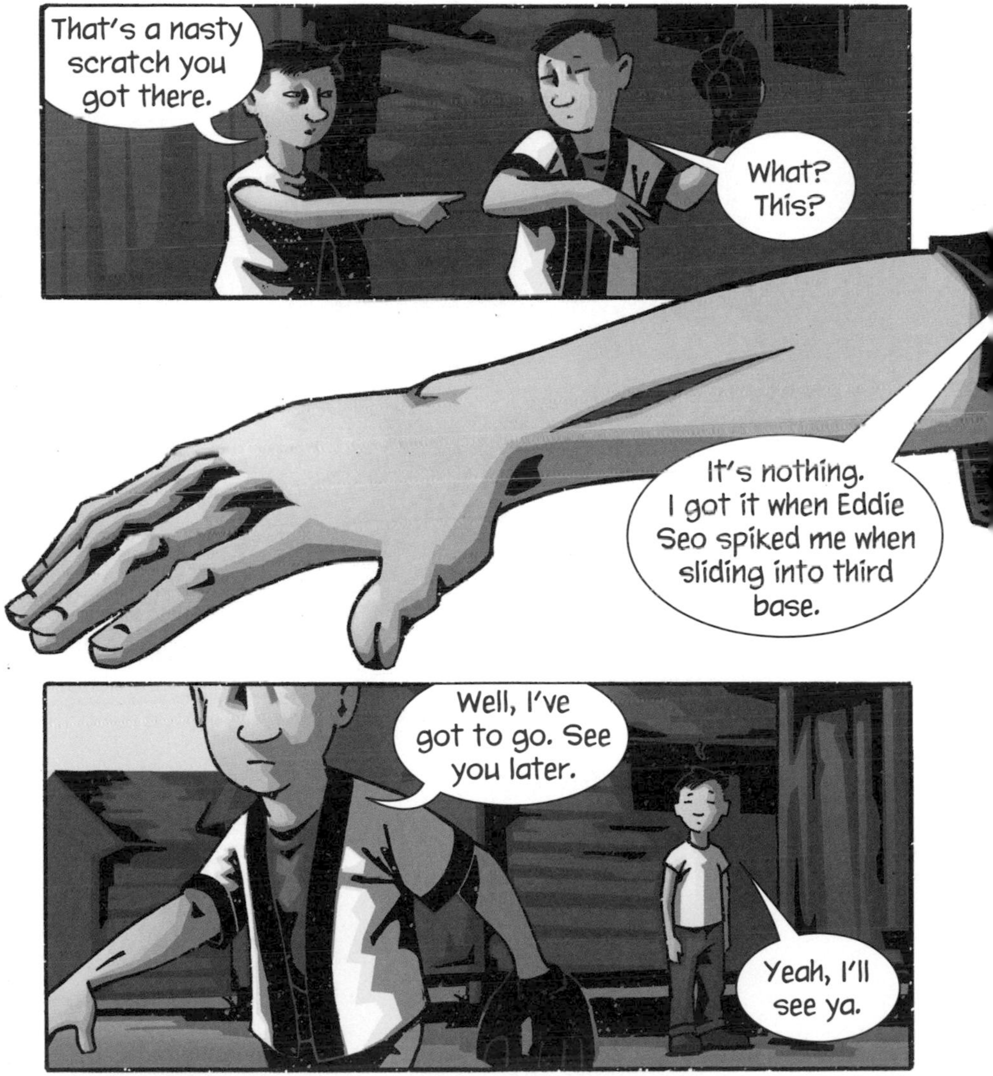
That's a nasty scratch you got there.
What? This?
It's nothing. I got it when Eddie Seo spiked me when sliding into third base.
Well, I've got to go. See you later.
Yeah, I'll see ya.

After talking to Joey, I continued on to John's barracks. He was surprised to see me.

"Tommy, what are you doing here?" John said, opening the door and pulling me inside.

"Trying to help you," I replied.

"You shouldn't be here," he said. "The head security officer doesn't want me talking to anyone until the case goes to trial."

"I just need to know a few things. Where were you when Mr. Sakata was attacked?" I asked.

"I had gone to your mess hall to see what movie was playing," he said. "It turned out to be a Gene Autry western. I stayed in the back for a while and then left. That's when I found the other guards searching my locker."

"Did you recognize anyone else at the movie?" I asked.

"Victor Kudo," John replied. "He denies seeing me there, even though I know he did. Without him, I have no proof."

"We'll see about that," I said, looking around the room.

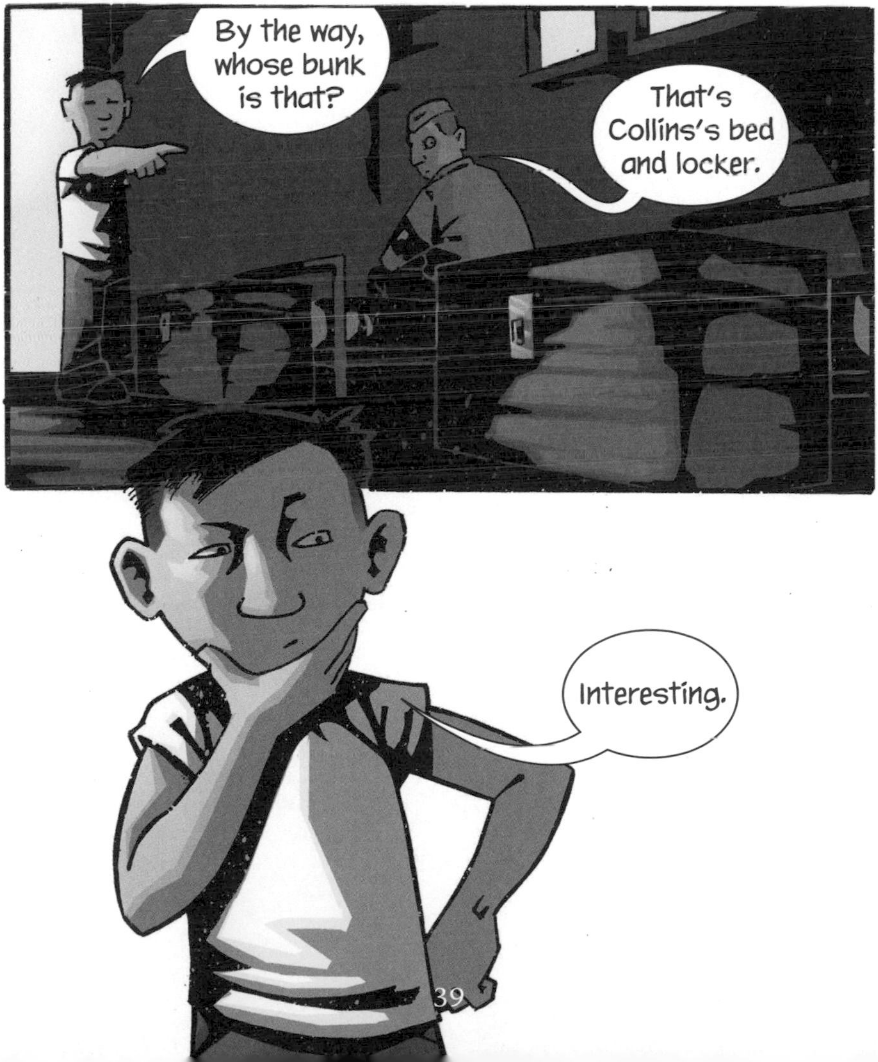
By the way, whose bunk is that?
That's Collins's bed and locker.
Interesting.

I had my first clue, but I wasn't sure what it meant. I knew I had to question the one person I didn't want to see again.

I walked across the street to the camp's youth social club. A group of older teens were playing basketball. I spotted Victor taking a breather near the sideline.

"Could I talk to you?" I asked him.

"What do you want?" Victor said.

"You were at the movie the night Mr. Sakata was attacked," I said. "John remembers seeing you there. Yet, you told the security officer you weren't there. You lied."

"So?" said Victor. He stood up and looked me in the eyes. I could see his bully friends approaching from behind.

I didn't back down. "Well, that would prove that John didn't do it," I said.

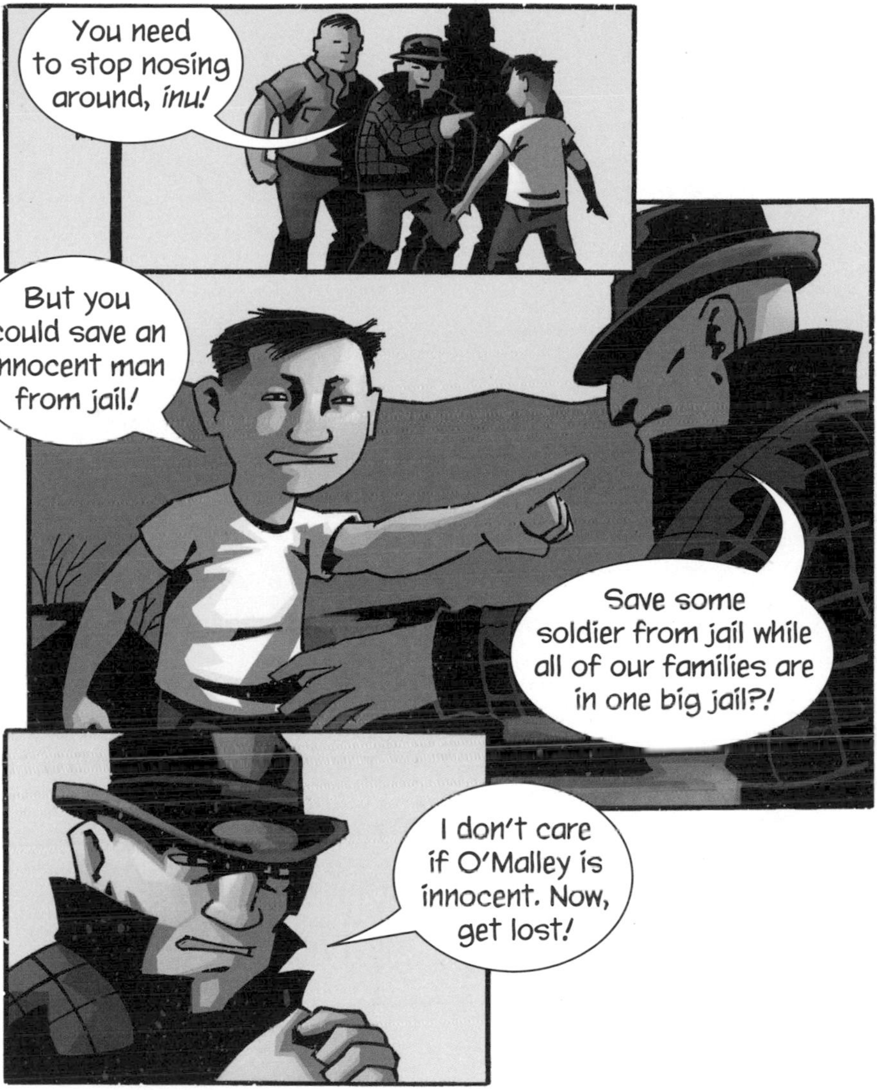
You need to stop nosing around, *inu!*
But you could save an innocent man from jail!
Save some soldier from jail while all of our families are in one big jail?!
I don't care if O'Malley is innocent. Now, get lost!

I was now pretty sure I knew what happened and why. After I left Victor, I double-checked a few things. Once I was confident that I knew the facts, I told the security officer my theory of the crime.

CHAPTER 6

Case Closed

The security officer asked everyone involved to meet in the mess hall after breakfast.

"You all know why you are here," the security officer said. "A crime has been committed and a guard stands accused.

"However, one person, Tommy Yamamoto, was determined to prove that Private John O'Malley was innocent. I did something a little unusual. I let Tommy poke around a bit. I figured he could find things out that I couldn't.

"Or, he would get tired and drop it. So you could imagine my surprise when he came to me last night and told me his theory. And now he is going to share it with you. Go ahead, Tommy."

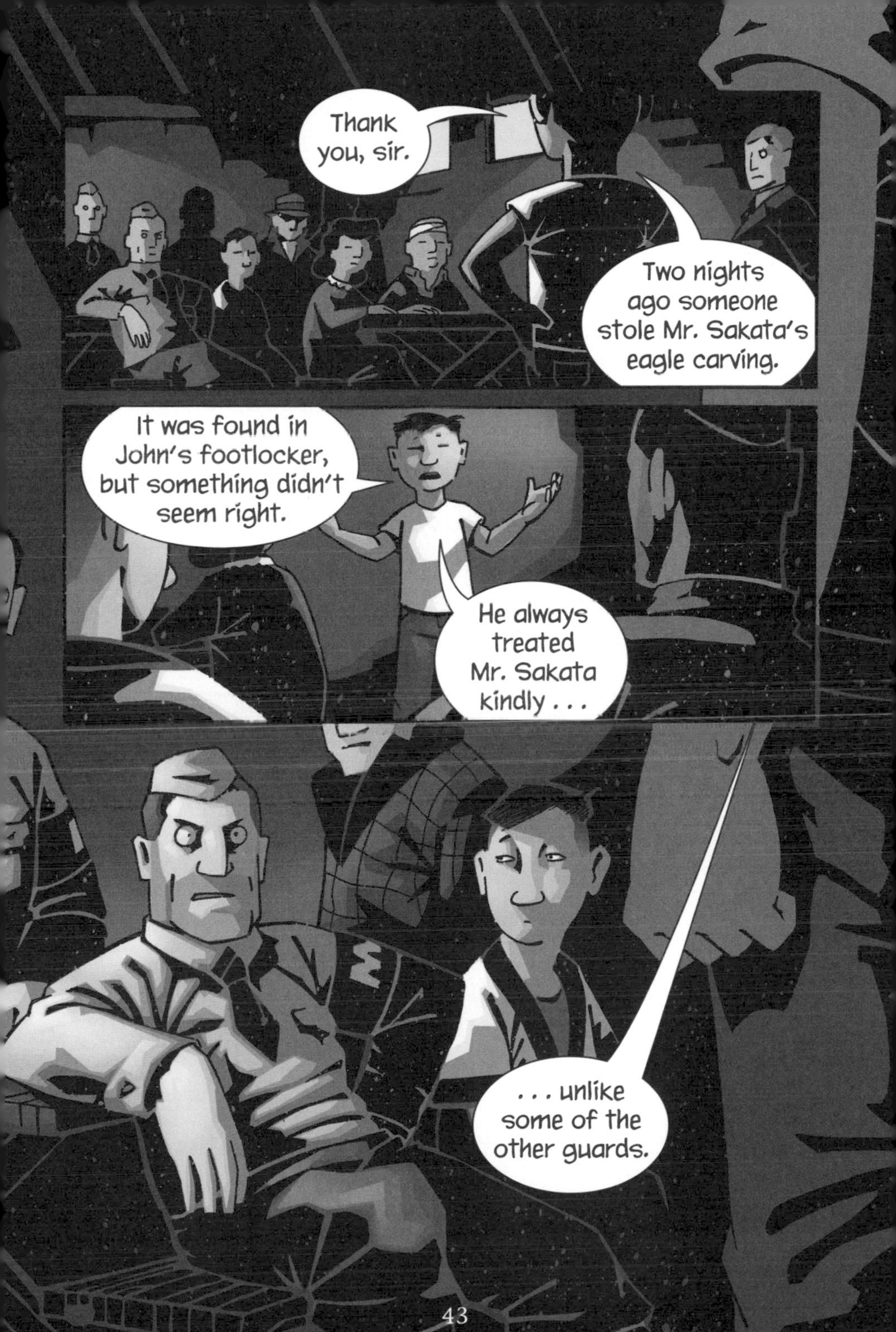
Thank you, sir.
Two nights ago someone stole Mr. Sakata's eagle carving.
It was found in John's footlocker, but something didn't seem right.
He always treated Mr. Sakata kindly . . .
. . . unlike some of the other guards.

"I didn't think it could be Mr. Collins," I continued. "He had never done anything violent before.

"When I went to visit John, I noticed that his bed and locker are right next to Collins's. That got me thinking," I said, continuing to circle the room. "What if someone was out to frame Collins but framed John by mistake?

"There are a lot of people in camp that were very happy to see a soldier in trouble. Victor Kudo came to mind. John told me that he saw Victor during the movie. Even though Victor denied it at first, he finally admitted that he saw John at the movies. So, they both couldn't have done it.

"At this point, I remembered something I read in the Sherlock Holmes novel, *The Sign of the Four*. Holmes tells Dr. Watson that when you have eliminated the impossible, whatever remains must be the truth."

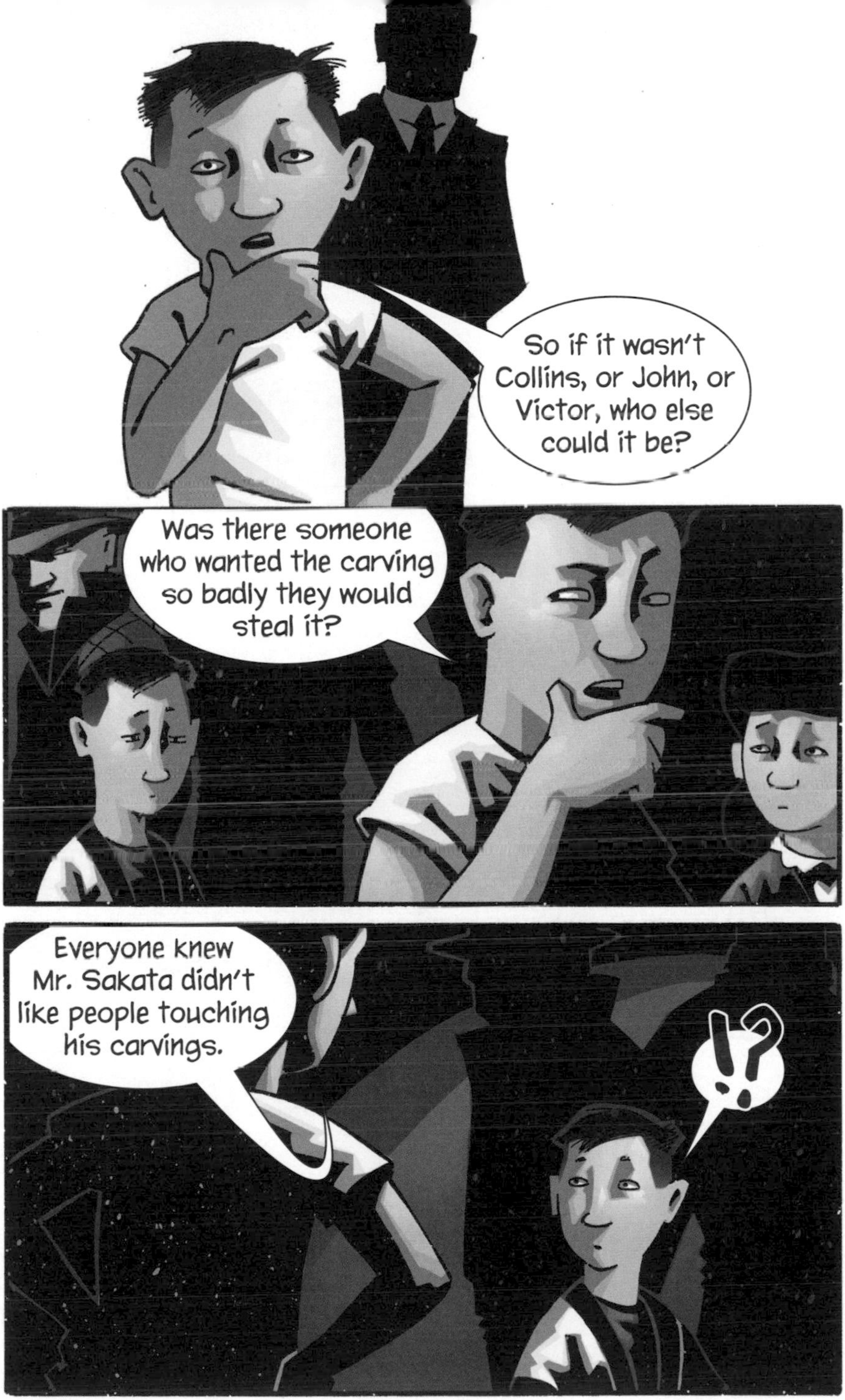
So if it wasn't Collins, or John, or Victor, who else could it be?
Was there someone who wanted the carving so badly they would steal it?
Everyone knew Mr. Sakata didn't like people touching his carvings.
!?

"I didn't do it!" Joey shouted.

"But all the pieces fit," I said. "You told me that you enjoyed the Roy Rogers movie. But that night, a Gene Autry western was shown instead. I know because I spoke with the person who ran the film that night."

"Then there is the cut above your wrist," I continued. "You said you got it playing baseball. But, the cut was already scabbed over when I saw it. I think you got the cut when you snuck up on Mr. Sakata and snatched the carving."

"It was an accident," replied Joey. "It was dark outside, and I had set my baseball bat down. Mr. Sakata tripped over it. When I saw him fall, I got scared and ran. I panicked and hid in the officer's barrack."

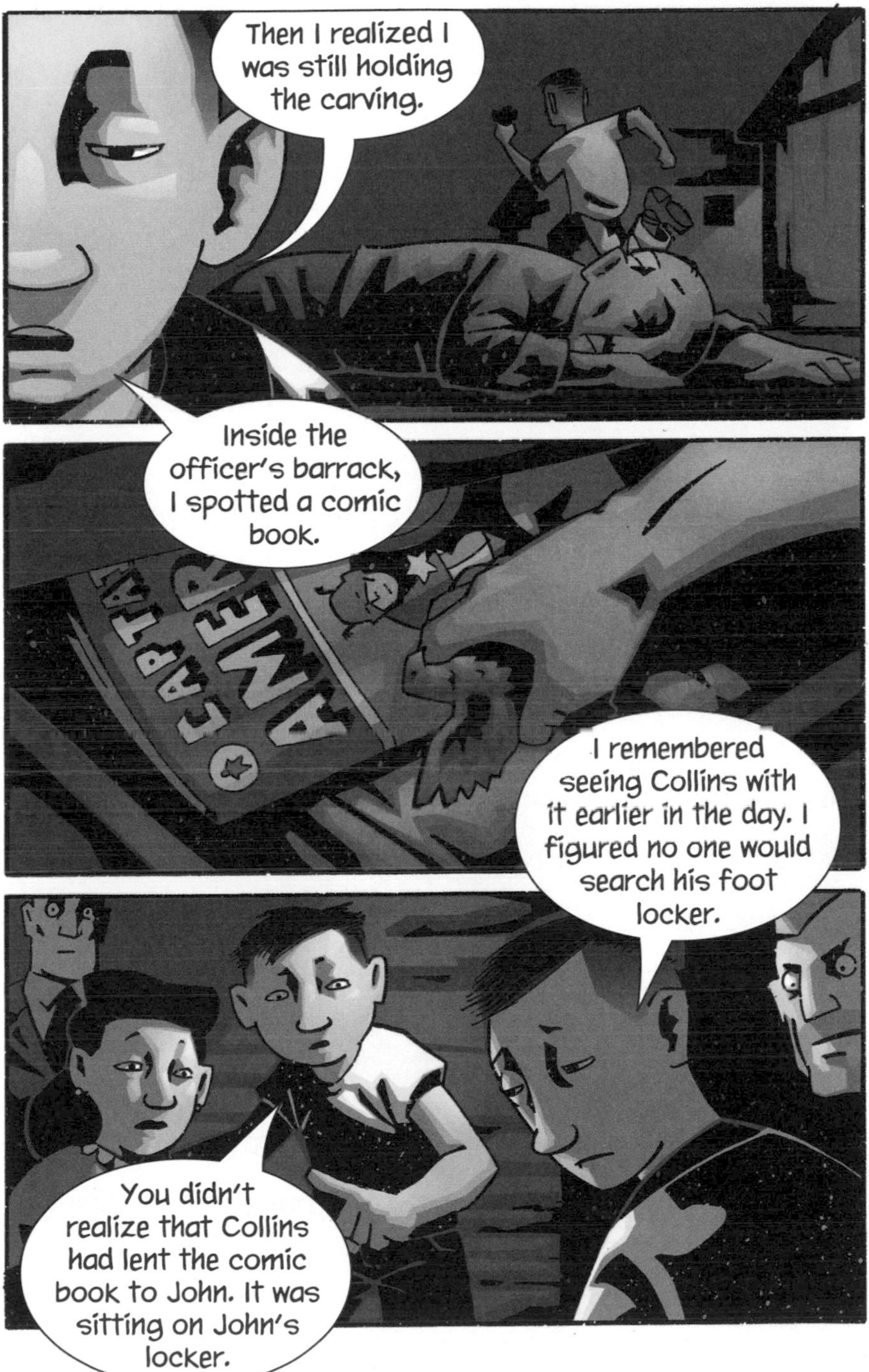

Then I realized I was still holding the carving.
Inside the officer's barrack, I spotted a comic book.
I remembered seeing Collins with it earlier in the day. I figured no one would search his foot locker.
You didn't realize that Collins had lent the comic book to John. It was sitting on John's locker.

"Yeah, Collins let me borrow it earlier that afternoon," John said.

"What's going to happen to Joey?" I asked the head officer.

"He will be confined to quarters for ninety days," he replied. "Of course, that does not include any punishment his parents give him. Do you understand, young man?"

"Yes, sir," Joey said. "I'm sorry for all the trouble I have caused."

"As for you Tommy, you should be proud of yourself," the head officer continued. "You stood up for a friend and did the right thing despite the trouble you faced for doing it."

"Thank you, sir," I said.

As the crowd began to leave the mess hall, I spotted my mother sitting in the back row. I didn't know she had come.

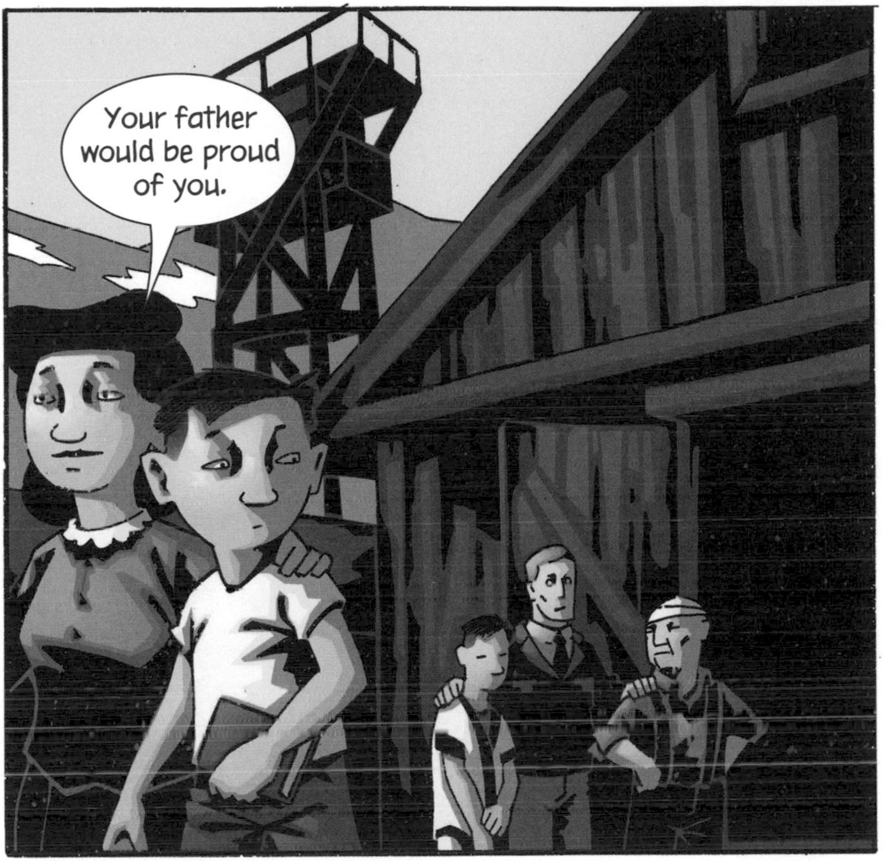
Your father would be proud of you.

I knew that some day my father would join us at camp. We would be a family again. Until then, my hero, Sherlock Holmes, would get me through the long days. Holmes helped people who were wrongly accused of crimes. At Manzanar, I learned just how important it was to stand up for innocence.

About the Author

Eric Fein is a freelance writer and editor. He has edited books for Marvel and DC Comics, which included well-known characters such as Batman, Superman, Wonder Woman, and Spider-Man. Fein has also written dozens of graphic novels and educational children's books. He currently lives in Ridgefield Park, New Jersey.

About the Illustrator

Before becoming an illustrator, Kurt Hartman had many jobs. He was a carpenter, a painter, a set dresser, an art director, a scenic artist for movies, a production designer, and much more. Today, he works as an illustrator and designer in Los Angeles, California. He lives with his wife Lauren, their children, Henry and Abigail, and far too many cats.

Glossary

agent (AY-juhnt)—an official who works for a government organization such as the FBI

barracks (BA-ruhks)—the buildings where military soldiers live

citizens (SIT-ih-zhuhz)—members of a country who have the right to live there

immigrant (IM-uh-gruhnt)—someone who has moved from one country to another country

infirmary (in-FUR-mur-ee)—a place where sick or injured people are cared for or treated

internment camp (IN-turn-muhnt CAMP)—a place used to hold suspected enemies during a war

investigation (in-VESS-tuh-gay-shuhn)—a close study of a crime to find out as much about the event as possible

quarters (KWOR-turz)—the lodging or rooms where people live, often during military combat

suspect (SUHSS-pekt)—someone thought to be responsible for committing a crime

More About the Manzanar Relocation Center

On December 7, 1941, Japanese planes attacked the U.S. Pacific Fleet on the island of Oahu, Hawaii. In less than two hours of fighting, 2,403 Americans died during the raid. One day later, December 8, 1941, President Franklin D. Roosevelt asked the U.S. Congress to declare war on Japan.

As the United States entered World War II (1939–1945), suspicion against Japanese Americans started to grow. Some people believed these citizens could really be spies working for the enemy, Japan. On February 19, 1942, President Roosevelt signed Executive Order 9066. The document allowed the U.S. military to remove potentially dangerous citizens from the West Coast.

In the following months, 120,000 Japanese Americans were forced from their homes. These innocent citizens were moved to ten different housing camps, often called internment camps or relocation centers. Many would be held there for the next four years.

Manzanar Relocation Center in the desert of California housed 11,070 Japanese Americans. As with other camps, more than half of these internees were children. Although these children still attended school, life for them was anything but normal. Their families were forced to share small rooms with other families. In some camps, residents had little food to eat and poor medical care. Temperatures in the desert could reach 110 degrees Fahrenheit (43 degrees Celsius).

Even with these challenges, life for Japanese Americans continued. While at Manzanar, 188 couples were married. Dozens of students received their college degrees. Some residents even served in the military, fighting for the United States in World War II.

Soon after the war ended, Manzanar Relocation Center closed on August 14, 1945. In 1992, the camp became a National Historic Site. Today, visitors can learn about the unfair treatment of these American citizens, and how they succeeded despite the obstacles.

Discussion Questions

1. During World War II (1939–1945), the United States government sent many Japanese Americans to relocation centers like Manzanar. The government believed they could be spies for Japan. How do you feel about this decision? Do you think it was wrong for the U.S. government to suspect all Japanese Americans of spying? Why or why not?

2. In the story, some of the guards at Manzanar treated people poorly. So why do you think Tommy wanted to help one of the guards? Would you have done the same?

3. In the end, Tommy's friend Joey turned out to be the thief. Do you think Tommy should have told on his best friend? If your friend committed a crime, would you tell on them?

Writing Prompts

1. This story is known as historical fiction. The historical event is true, but the characters are fictional. Choose your favorite historical event. Then make up a story that happens on that day.

2. At the end of the book, Tommy believes he will be reunited with his father soon. What do you think? Write a story about what happens next.

3. Write your own mystery. Who will solve the case? Who will be the suspects? And who will be the real criminal? It's up to you!

Internet Sites

Do you want to know more about subjects related to this book? Or are you interested in learning about other topics? Then check out FactHound, a fun, easy way to find Internet sites.

Our investigative staff has already sniffed out great sites for you!

Here's how to use FactHound:

1. Visit *www.facthound.com*

2. Select your grade level.

3. To learn more about subjects related to this book, type in the book's ISBN number: **9781434207517.**

4. Click the **Fetch It** button.

FactHound will fetch the best Internet sites for you.